Shifty McGifty
AND
SLIPPERY SAM
Jingle Bells!

TRACEY CORDEROY
STEVEN LENTON

nosy crow

First published in the UK in 2017 by Nosy Crow Ltd
The Crow's Nest, 14 Baden Place, Crosby Row,
London, SE1 1YW, UK

Nosy Crow and associated logos are trademarks and/or registered
trademarks of Nosy Crow Ltd

3 5 7 9 10 8 6 4 2

A CIP catalogue record for this book will be available from the British Library.

Printed in Spain

Papers used by Nosy Crow are made from wood grown in
sustainable forests.

ISBN: 978 0 85763 962 2

www.nosycrow.com

CONTENTS

Jingle Bells!   5

Sea-Monster Ahoy!   41

The Lucky Cat!   81

Jingle Bells!

Chapter One

"I LOVE Christmas!" twinkled Sam, draping even *more* decorations around the café.

It was Christmas Eve morning. Snow was falling softly and the café was buzzing with customers. Fred was happily wolfing down sugar mice, while Rover feasted on mince pies, and Scottie had been scoffing shortbread stars for hours!

As Shifty appeared with some candy-cane

biscuits, the café phone started to ring.

Sam answered it.

"Hello? Oh *really*?" he cried. "Yes! No problem! A-and *thank you*!"

Shifty strolled over. "Who was that?" he asked.

"SANTA!" beamed Sam, his eyes wide. "He wants US to make him a Christmas cake!"

"AMAZING!" cried Shifty. "Hang on – for when?"

Sam swallowed hard. "This afternoon."

"But Sam!" Shifty checked the clock. "That's *soon*!"

With that, Duchess patted Shifty's arm.

"Don't worry," she said, "if anyone can do it, *you* two can!"

"We c-can?" Shifty spluttered.

"We CAN!" grinned Sam.

"LET'S GET BAKING!"

The rest of the morning was *crazy*. Mixers whirred, spoons beat, and piping bags oozed white icing. And against all the odds, just after lunch…

"You DID it!"

everyone cheered.

Santa's cake was a masterpiece and the boys were so proud.

"Right, time to deliver it!" Shifty smiled. "*To the Bakemobile!*"

Leaving Fred in charge of the café, they threw on their scarves and woolly hats. But as they carried the cake to the van, who should they see doing tricks on his snowboard but their annoying next-door neighbour – Red Rocket.

B4KE 1

"Oi! Who's that *cake* for?"

he called, whooshing up.

"Santa!"
smiled Shifty.
"We're taking
it to him now."
"He'll
definitely get stuck
up the chimney if he
eats ALL that!" said Red
Rocket. He gave a cheeky
snigger but the boys ignored him.
"So ... anyway," said Sam as they
got in the van. "We'd better be off.
Happy Christmas!"

"Yeah, Happy Christmas," scoffed Red Rocket. "To ME!"

Shifty wound down his window. "You'd better stop being naughty," he warned. "Or Santa won't leave you any presents!"

"Don't care," shrugged Red Rocket, though he spoke very quietly, with his fingers tightly crossed behind his back.

He turned and whooshed off down the road, making a very RUDE noise over his shoulder.

"Pthhhhhhh!!!"

Chapter
Two

The journey to Lapland began. Sam was in charge of directions.

"Go *south*," he nodded, spreading out their huge map.

"But Lapland's at the *North* Pole?" said Shifty. "Oh, Sam – you've got the map *upside-down*."

"Ooops – sorry!"

Sam soon got bored of map-reading and

told Christmassy jokes
instead. He had thousands.
In fact, he'd been thinking
them up *all year*...

"What does Jack Frost like best about school?"

"I dunno," said Shifty.

"SNOW and tell!"

"What did one snowman say to the other?" said Sam.

"I dunno," said Shifty.

"Hey, can you smell *carrots*?!"

Sam was so busy laughing that he could hardly tell his next joke.

"What b-bird is R-REALLY good at writing?" he chortled.

"I dunno," said Shifty.

"A PEN-guin!"

Though Shifty said Sam's jokes were GREAT, he definitely thought he should *save* some for Christmas Day.

So, instead, Sam cheerily set about singing the *only* Christmas song he knew. He sang it. And sang it. And SANG it *until*—

"Time for the Christmas QUIET GAME!"
yelled Shifty. "You start."

But Sam wasn't great at the quiet game.
There were *so* many *things* to point out.
Sam didn't want Shifty missing all the jolly
Christmas *scenery*...

"Hey, look at that super-cool SNOWMAN!"
cried Sam. "He's such an unusual shape."

"Mmmm," replied Shifty, his eyes still fixed
on the road.

Shifty drove a bit further and…

"SHIFTY!" called Sam. "Aww, cute little puppy carol-singers!"

Well, most of them were cute. And teeny-tiny. All except one. "Who I *think*," snorted Sam, "looks a little too fond of mince pies if you ask me!"

Going further north the weather was
freezing. After a long, long journey, they
finally got to Lapland, and Shifty pulled
up outside Santa's log cabin. It looked so
pretty. Like a big iced gingerbread house!

Shifty and Sam got out of the van and
were admiring Santa's fairy lights around
his front door when—Splat!

A freezing cold snowball whacked Sam
on the bottom.

"Ow – Shifty – there was no need for
that!"

"It wasn't me!" Shifty spluttered.

"Oh yes it was!"
"Oh no it WASN'T!"
"Oh yes it was!"
"Oh no it—"
BUT THEN, THE DOOR TO
SANTA'S CABIN BEGAN
TO OPEN...

Chapter
Three

"Boys!" beamed Santa Paws, welcoming them in. "Such a splendid cake! Do come and sit by the fire."

In trotted three little elves with afternoon tea for everyone.

When they were full of tea and marshmallows, Santa showed the boys his Christmas workshop.

His elves were making the last few Christmas presents to add to the huge pile already waiting on Santa's sleigh in his big stone barn.

"Wow!" said Shifty. "They look busy!" Some

elves were sewing, while others sawed and hammered, and a team were wrapping all the gifts. There were ribbons, and bows, and glittery gift-tags everywhere!

23

"Oh, yes!" nodded Santa. "Well, you see, I'll be setting off very soon. SO many toys to deliver!" he nodded. "Like to see my sleigh?"

"Yes please!" cried Sam.

So Santa took them out to his big stone barn.

"Are there reindeers in there?" Shifty whispered.

"Of course," smiled Santa. "And my sleigh, brimming with presents!"

Santa opened the barn door and the boys looked in. But their faces fell. All the presents, and Santa's sack too, were gone!

"But how?" cried Santa.

Shifty gasped. "Someone must have stolen them!" he said.

"Look!" Sam pointed. "Pawprints in the snow – there!"

"And *whoosh*-prints," Shifty nodded. They were just like the marks a SNOWBOARD would make.

"It's him!" shouted Sam, and Shifty gave a nod.

"RED ROCKET!"

With that, they saw him
snowboarding off in the direction
of the trees.

"He's in his silly cape!" Sam
cried.

"After him!"

Santa told the boys they'd be faster on his sleigh.

So in they jumped and away they went, with Shifty at the reins.

"Red Rocket!" yelled Sam.
"You give back those presents!"

But back came a cheeky voice,
"Make me, losers!
Ptthhhhhh!"

The race was on. "We'll
catch him!" cried Shifty.

"But he *is* really fast," replied Sam.

"Come on, reindeers!" Shifty called, and Sam
kept tossing them Santa's marshmallows as fuel.

The sleigh picked up speed, weaving
through the trees. They were getting closer and
closer! Red Rocket looked like a fluffy teddy
bear with a sack twice his size on his back!

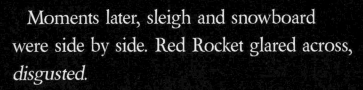

Moments later, sleigh and snowboard
were side by side. Red Rocket glared across,
disgusted.

"Oi! Stop CROWDING me – road hogs!"
he glowered. So Shifty overtook him and
skidded to a halt, right in the path
of his snowboard.

"Arrgh!" Red Rocket screeched to a halt too and began to bumble off with the presents. But he was far too tubby to run very fast, and soon the boys had him caught. Sam grabbed Santa's sack.

"Don't snatch!" fumed Red Rocket. "You big Christmas meanies! That's RUDE. Well, don't expect a Christmas card from *me*. 'Cos I'm NEVER going to speak to *you* two EVER AGAIN!"

Chapter Four

"Couldn't you just tell Santa it was a *mistake*?" said Red Rocket, looking up with big eyes.

"I thought you weren't speaking to us," replied Shifty.

"Oh bother!" Red Rocket stamped his furry little foot. "I forgot."

When they took him to Santa, Red Rocket was in a big sulk. But finally he did tell the truth…

"OK, I did it! But *only* because Giraffe-neck – I mean *Shifty* – said I wouldn't get any *presents* if I was naughty. Which I *kind of* have been, quite a lot this year. By mistake…"

"Well," Santa said, "what must you do instead of being naughty, do you think?"

"Errr," frowned Red Rocket. "That's hard… Try to be *good*?"

Santa nodded.

"Cool!" cried Red Rocket. "So that's what I'll be – EVERY day! Soooo … can I have a *present* now?

A quite big one…?"

Before Santa could answer, Shifty gave a shout from where he'd been loading presents on to the sleigh.

"Uh-oh," he cried. "We must have hit a rock when we were chasing Red Rocket. The sleigh is broken!"

"Oh dear!" gasped Santa. "Whatever will I do? No one will have any *toys* in the morning unless we mend it, and quick!"

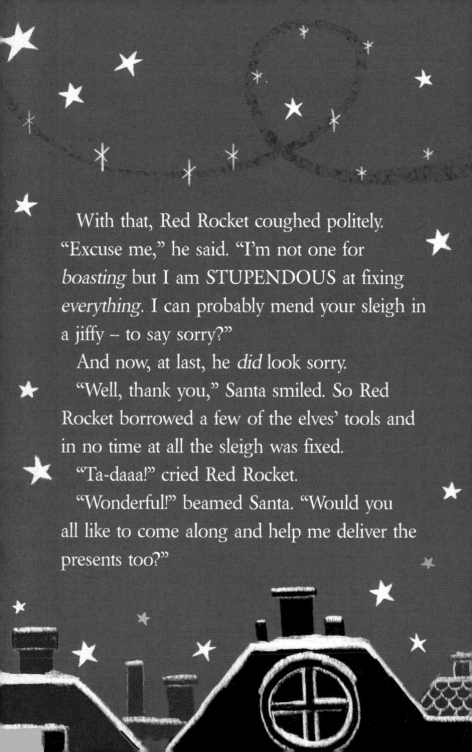

With that, Red Rocket coughed politely. "Excuse me," he said. "I'm not one for *boasting* but I am STUPENDOUS at fixing *everything*. I can probably mend your sleigh in a jiffy – to say sorry?"

And now, at last, he *did* look sorry.

"Well, thank you," Santa smiled. So Red Rocket borrowed a few of the elves' tools and in no time at all the sleigh was fixed.

"Ta-daaa!" cried Red Rocket.

"Wonderful!" beamed Santa. "Would you all like to come along and help me deliver the presents too?"

"Oooo,
yes PLEASE!"
everyone cried.
"Hooray!"
They jumped in the
sleigh and soared off through
the stars. And what a magical
night it was too! Delivering
presents was quite the best
thing EVER.

When the very last present was under the last tree, Santa asked if anyone would like a piece of Shifty and Sam's Christmas cake as a reward for all their hard work.

They all turned to the back of the sleigh to fetch it. But everyone gave a gasp! For *who* should they see already there, icing all OVER his face, but...

"Ooops!" blushed Red Rocket. "I should have waited, right?

Burrrp!"

Sea-Monster Ahoy!

"Ahhh, isn't this GREAT!" giggled Shifty as the waves tickled his toes.

"Sure is," smiled Sam, splashing him. "Wheee!"

The boys were on holiday at the seaside, staying at **Puffin Pete's Campsite.** Tomorrow it was "Fun Day!" at the beach, with a funfair and a marching band. There were going to be lots of competitions too!

Shifty and Sam were entering the sea-fishing competition. They were just starting to practise when suddenly one of the other fishermen shouted,

"Sea-Monster!"

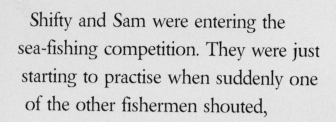

It was Spug, a chubby little pug. He was staying at their campsite too. Spug was standing on the rock he'd been fishing from, pointing out to sea. But there was no monster in sight.

"You're seeing things!" Shifty
called.

Spug shook his head. "No! I did
see a monster! I swear!"

A small crowd had gathered on the
sand, having heard Spug's worried
cries. Spug and the boys went to join
them.

"So, what did this monster look
like?" gasped a kite-flying collie.

Spug's eyes widened. "Really mean! Its hair was a tangle of sea-serpents and it had evil sticky-out eyes. And the biggest SHARK fin on its back you've ever seen!"

Little Ern, a skinny whippet pup, said he'd seen *the very* same thing yesterday. His dad, Bigger Ern, nodded. "He *did* say that."

Suddenly Puffin Pete raced up. The news of the monster had travelled fast.

"You know what this means," Pete said with a sigh. "Tomorrow's Fun Day will have to be cancelled. The Mayor won't have folk visiting with a *monster* on the loose!" Pete added that

no Fun Day would be really
bad news. "The town will lose money.
And I will too. All my campers will pack
up and leave!" he said, looking worried.

That afternoon a special meeting was
called in Sally Seagull's Tearoom in the
old lighthouse. It turned out that Puffin
Pete was right.

"I'm sorry," said the Mayor, "but tomorrow's Fun Day is off."

Pete looked really disappointed. And he wasn't the only one.

The marching band had been practising for *ages*. The freshly painted funfair rides were gleaming.

And Speedy Reg, a VERY
slooooooow tortoise, had even given
his crazy-golf course a makeover.

He tutted sadly. "It's taken me a whole
YEAR to stick up that bunting!"

47

Chapter Two

"Psst – *Pete!*" whispered Shifty. "Me and Sam can sort this out. We're ever so good at catching baddies!"

Sam finished his "sad-news doughnut" and grinned.

"Yeah, catching sea-monsters for us is a *piece of cake!*"

Pete looked surprised, but grateful too. "Well, thank you, boys!" he said.

"But best just keep the plan to *ourselves*," Shifty whispered.

He said they'd need some bits and bobs to help them with the capture – like a *really* strong fishing rod and a jolly BIG net.

Luckily Pete had a boatshed. "I used to fish a lot once," he said. "I've got tons of useful bits in there – come and see!"

They sneaked outside and Pete hurried them along to his boatshed on the jetty. As he unlocked the door, he smiled.

"Ahhh," Pete said. "I haven't been down here for ages. Feels good to be back!"

He led the way in and the boys looked around.

"Oh, wow!" Sam cried. "This is great!"
There were rods and reels of all sizes, and
torches that flashed different colours. And
Pete's super-big fishing nets looked perfect
for catching a sea-monster!

They took what they needed, then Pete led them outside. "And you're going to want a *boat*," he said.

He nodded to the jetty, where his old fishing boat was tied up with a big, thick rope.

"She's called *The Salty Seadog*," Pete said
with a smile. "And she's yours to borrow – if
you'd like?"

"Wow!" cried Shifty, and Sam gave a squeal.
"I've always wanted to be a pirate!"

Pete said she'd need some sprucing up. "She's a little rusty and worn."

"Don't worry," said Shifty. "If me and Sam work hard she'll be shipshape again in no time."

"And of course I'll help too!" beamed Pete, his eyes twinkling.

They got to work right away. There wasn't a minute to lose! Sam

scrubbed *The Salty Seadog*'s deck, Shifty fixed
any broken timbers and Pete wiped down the
crow's nest until...

"Time to go!" Shifty cried.

It was nightfall and a mist was creeping over the sea as Shifty steered *The Salty Seadog* out of the harbour. Sam kept lookout from the crow's nest.

"Shiver me timbers, sea-monster," he giggled. "We're COMING!"

Chapter
Three

But as the boys sailed further out to sea, huge foamy gusts rocked the boat.

Sam wasn't smiling *now*. The night was black and the swirly white mist looked like GHOSTS!

"A-as we've not seen a **S-SINGLE** sea-m-monster," Sam quivered, "I t-think Spug was **WRONG**, d-don't you?"

"Absolutely!" gulped Shifty. "I'm s-sure there is NO SUCH THING!"

Big punchy waves were thumping the boat. Being pirates, Sam thought, was really soggy! "M-maybe we should just go back?" he said.

But, thanks to the thick mist, Shifty wasn't sure which way *was* back!

"We're n-not lost, though!" Shifty shivered, trying to peer through the mist. "Just, um … exploring."

Sam groaned as Shifty sailed on a bit more. More mist. More soggy. More rocking side-to-side and UP and down.

"SHIFTY!" Sam wailed, rubbing his tummy. "I think I've caught pirate-lurgy! My tummy hurts. And *whoa* – hang on – I don't even fancy a *doughnut*. I think I'm … *dying!*"

Shifty said that Sam was just seasick, and he handed him an old bucket.

"And we're STILL not lost!" Shifty added quickly. "But we do need to sail around for a *tiny* bit more..."

A REALLY loooooooooooooooooooong time later...

"Hey, Sam!" cried Shifty. "It's morning!"

Sam's head popped up out of his sick bucket. "Phew! At last!"

As they passed Spug's fishing rock, Sam *even* managed a *smile*. They were almost back, and in one *piece* too!

But then he saw it! Sea-serpent-y
hair, sticky-out eyes and … a shark fin!
Slowly, Sam pointed a small
shaky paw…

"SEA-MONSTER!"

Shifty yelled for Sam to cast
the net and Sam did it right
away. It hit the water with a
great big

splash!

"Did we get the monster?"
Shifty cried.

"I'm not sure!" shouted
Sam. "I think so!"

They chugged back to shore and examined their catch, still wriggling about in the net.

"Wait!" gasped Sam. And Shifty looked closer.

"What's THAT?!"

The sea-monster was just a cute baby seal wearing a sea-monster *costume*! Its sea-serpent-y hair was seaweed, its sticky-out eyes were seashells and its shark-fin was just a pointy piece of driftwood.

"But why," frowned Shifty as the baby seal blushed, "were you trying to *scare* everyone?"

Chapter Four

The little seal looked up at the boys with big, round eyes.

"Awww, you're so cute," said Sam.

"And *that's* why I did it," sniffed the baby seal – whose name, he told them, was Ollie.

"I don't *want* to be *cute*. I want to be *big*. Big like my brothers! So I thought, if I dressed up as a *monster*, and scared everyone, my brothers would think I was TOUGH and

COOL. Like them."

Shifty and Sam nodded. They understood how he felt. But this Fun Day was so important for the *town*.

"How about we ask," Shifty said, "if you can be part of the Fun Day?"

"A pretend-sea-monster-catching competition!" cried Sam.

"Oh, I'd *love* that!" Ollie beamed. "Would you ask for me – *pleeeease*?"

The boys smiled back at the little seal. "Sure thing!"

They hurried off to see the Mayor before it was too late. If they were going to save this Fun Day they had to be QUICK!

At ten o'clock, crowds gathered at the beach. The Fun Day was back ON!

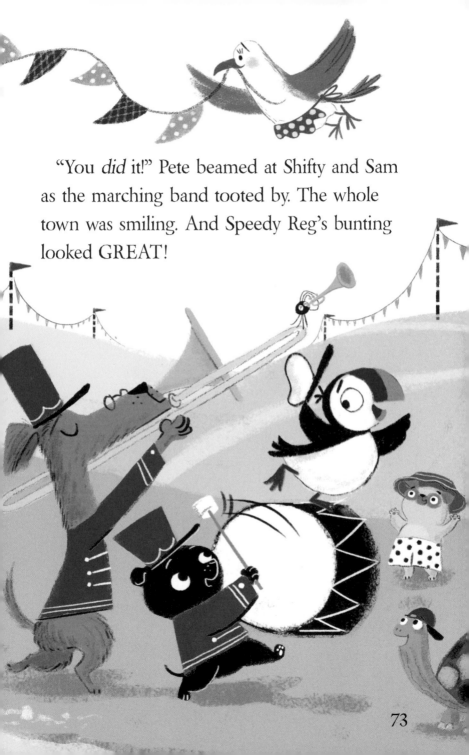

"You *did* it!" Pete beamed at Shifty and Sam as the marching band tooted by. The whole town was smiling. And Speedy Reg's bunting looked GREAT!

The boys spent the
morning at the funfair.

Then in the afternoon it was competition time!

Colin the collie won the kite-flying, Maisy Mole won best sandcastle (with mile-long moat!). And the crazy-golf was won by Dylan, a friendly golden retriever, who even brought back all the golf balls at the end!

But the pretend-sea-monster-catching competition was easily the most exciting and fun. Ollie, now back in his costume, dodged the catchers' nets with ease.

"Grrr," he giggled, trying to look tough. "I have fierce hair and fierce eyes and a huge fierce fin on my back! And I'll gobble you up with my snippy-snap jaws – rahhhhhh!"

"You tell 'em, Ollie!" his big brothers cheered, watching on.

After much splashing and swishing of nets, the little seal let Spug the pug catch him. He liked the look of Spug because *he* was little too!

"Yay!" beamed Spug, throwing his paws around Ollie.

"PUG-HUG!"

The Lucky Cat!

"Look, Shifty!" beamed Sam, hurrying up with a wonky-tailed, bug-eyed cat. "I've just bought this LUCKY cat!"

Shifty looked at the chipped china ornament Sam was waving.

"Er, nice!"

The boys had been serving refreshments at a local car boot sale. But so far the day had not gone well. First, they'd had a flat tyre on the way. Then they'd hardly sold any cakes.

"But our luck will soon change with this
TREASURE!" nodded Sam. "I think I'll call
him Brian!"

That night, back at the café, Sam sat Brian by the till. "There!" He patted its ugly head. "Make us LUCKY!"

Shifty and Sam had lots to do before they went to bed. They needed to be ready for the breakfast rush in the morning.

While Shifty baked muffins, Sam swept the floor. He liked sweeping because he could move around. Up to the fridge, for instance, where he always liked to check INSIDE for dust – and (when Shifty wasn't looking) snaffle some of Shifty's new block of "strictly-NOT-for-Sam-but-totally-irresistible" cheese!

Soon the muffins were baked. Shifty passed
them to Sam to pop on to a cooling rack.
And this *would* have worked *well* had Sam
not tripped up (just as he walked past Brian),
causing the muffins to fly out of the tin.

The boys held their breath as the muffins
headed towards the nice clean table, and the
cooling rack. But then, at the last minute, they
ran out of steam, right over the DUST pile
Sam had just finished sweeping, and—

POOF!

Sam peered down at the
hairy grey lumps. "Doh,
unlucky!" he sighed.

"Hmm!" grunted Shifty, rolling his sleeves up to start AGAIN.

While Shifty did that, Sam made their bedtime cocoa, plonking down the milk-frothing machine next to Brian.

"Watch *this* then, lucky kitty!" Sam exclaimed. "Hey, Shifty!" he called. "Bet our milk's extra lovely with *Brian* watching over things tonight!"

Beaming, Sam turned on the frothing machine. But the lid must have not been *quite* clipped on, and...

"Oh Sam!!" Shifty groaned and they both started mopping up the mess. But as they did, they clean forgot about Shifty's *second* batch of muffins now BURNING TO BITS!

"Er, Shifty – smoke!" Sam pointed.

"Oh no!" yelled Shifty, rushing over to the oven. Yet MORE muffins ruined!

He glared from the smoky black dollops to Sam, and then across to bug-eyed *Brian*.

"Some lucky cat *he* is!" Shifty puffed. "Sam – bed – before anything *else* goes wrong!" Shifty plodded up the stairs. And, after snaffling more cheese, Sam followed him.

Chapter
Two

Next morning the café was buzzing with customers, all showing off their car boot sale "treasures".

"I got this back-scratcher! Nearly new!" beamed Hercules, giving Rover's hairy back a little scratch.

"Well!" Lady Woofington

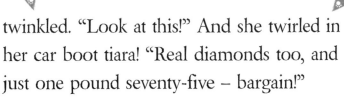

twinkled. "Look at this!" And she twirled in her car boot tiara! "Real diamonds too, and just one pound seventy-five – bargain!"

"What did *you* get, Shifty?" Scottie asked.

Shifty pointed at Brian. "Sam's bought a 'lucky' cat," he said. "Problem is, we've had BAD luck ever since."

With that, who should plod downstairs but Sam. And did he look rough today! He had great big bags under his eyes, and instead of wearing his normal chef's clothes…

"Are those your bedroom curtains?!" giggled Hercules.

"Eh?" Sam muttered, looking down.

"Gosh!" Scottie tutted. "He must have ripped them clean off the rail!"

Sam plodded away to serve customers.
But that didn't go well either.

"I asked for coffee – not toffee!" Duchess
frowned. And Scottie had ordered a *Victoria*
sponge not a *bath* sponge!

If Shifty had thought Sam was muddly last night, it was nothing like he was today!

"Psst, *Shifty*!" whispered Scottie. "Do you think that cat's *cursed*? Making bad things happen to its new owner, *Sam*!"

"No!" Shifty shook his head. "D-don't be daft! Sam just needs a little *rest.*"

They turned to see Sam now slapping icing on to Big-Eared Bob's fluffy head.

"My teddy's not a cupcake!" Scottie roared. But Sam wasn't listening as he popped a cherry on top.

"There!"

Shifty tried to make Sam take a break but Sam flatly refused. So the day passed slowly with muddle after muddle and a steady stream of broken cups and plates. By closing time the café was a MESS.

That night, as Shifty did his evening chores, he found Sam, broom in hand, sleeping like a puppy with his head in the fridge near the cheese.

What if Scottie was right, Shifty thought. *What if Brian was cursed?*

Something, after all, must be causing Sam's bonkers behaviour!

"Right…" Shifty muttered, helping Sam upstairs. Something HAD to be done.

If things didn't get better tomorrow, that wonky-tailed moggy was *going!*

"Duchess! What's the matter?" Shifty gasped as Duchess appeared for breakfast next day.

"I've been robbed!" cried Duchess. "AS I SLEPT! *Someone* went and stole my BEST PINK BLOOMERS off my washing line!"

"No!"

"I know!" Duchess fumed. And, it seemed, she wasn't the *only* one cross…

"Never mind her bloomin' bloomers!" puffed
Fred. "While *I* was sleeping, someone went
and trampled all over my prize pansies!"

"And broke my fence!" Rover boomed
holding up a broken bit. "Look!"

"Yes, but who'd do it though?" asked Fred.
"Pranksters!" cried Duchess. "Folk up to no
good! There must be a gang of practical
jokers in town."

With that, who should plod in
but Sam, looking EVEN more
dreadful than yesterday! And
although he wasn't wearing his
curtains today, his white chef's hat
had turned pink in the wash.

   Or had it…?

"My bloomers!"

cried Duchess. "Kindly take them off your HEAD!"

"YOUR WHAT?!" Sam gulped, whipping them off and peering at the bloomers in disgust.

"How did *these* get into my drawer?" he spluttered. "I have no idea where they came from – I, I PROMISE!"

The customers all agreed. Clearly Sam had been *set up* by this new gang of night-time pranksters!

Scottie, however, wasn't too sure. Nor was Shifty, who glared at Brian. Now that cat was cursing his *customers* too.

Enough was enough!

Sweeping Brian up, Shifty stuffed him behind a big bushy plant on the fridge. The moment Sam went to sleep that night, Brian was off to his brand-new home in the DUSTBIN!

That night, Sam could barely summon the energy to pinch a supper-time chunk of cheese. But he managed it. Just. While Shifty washed up at the sink.

"*Ahhhhhh! I've never been so tired!*" yawned Sam.

"Bed then," said Shifty. "Chop chop!"

The sooner Sam was tucked up and snoring, the sooner "OPERATION CAT DUMP" could begin!

Chapter Four

While Shifty waited for Sam to fall asleep, he slipped into his own bed to keep warm.

Problem was, it was really cosy. All soft and snuggly and nice. And no sooner had Shifty's head hit the pillow than—

"Zzzzzz…"

Shifty was dreaming about his big block of cheese when he was woken by noises from downstairs.

"What's that?!" He froze, listening hard.
Yep. Downstairs there were *definitely* noises.
"Uh-oh! ROBBERS!" he whispered.
Shifty crept out of bed and tiptoed into
Sam's room. Hmmm. Sam wasn't there.

He must have heard the robbers too,
thought Shifty, *and has already gone down to*
investigate.
Shifty slunk downstairs. It was very dark as
he edged through the café door. He felt along
the wall for the light switch.

And then Shifty felt
something very odd –
like a great big bushy
beard!

"AHHHH!" he cried, leaping back, but taking the beard with him. With that, he heard an enormous

THUNK!

Then a very sleepy cry.

"OW! My HEAD! That REALLY hurt! Is it morning?"

Shifty knew that voice. He flicked on the light.

"SAM!" gasped Shifty.

"Shifty??" Sam replied. "I was in bed – fast asleep – and now I'm here. How come?"

Shifty wasn't sure. Then he noticed the fridge and thought of his big chunk of cheese.

"Oh Sam! I think you've been sleepwalking!" cried Shifty. "Have you been eating CHEESE again?"

Cheese ALWAYS made Sam sleepwalk; that's why he wasn't allowed to eat Shifty's!

"Um…" Sam blushed.

"*Well?*" Shifty frowned. "Today? Yesterday?

Or every day – or NIGHT – this week?!"

Still blushing, Sam said, "Well, now that you *mention* it, I might have had a teeny bit."

Shifty tutted. "Huh! That's why you've been so *sleepy* all week! When you *should* have been *fast asleep in bed*, you've been UP – sleepwalking instead."

"I don't remember!" squeaked Sam. "But my clumsiness and mistakes—"

"All because you were so *sleepy...*" replied Shifty. "And Duchess's bloomers! And Fred's pansies – and Rover's garden fence."

"That was *me*?" Sam gave a gasp and Shifty nodded back.

"All while you were sleepwalking," Shifty said. "And we'd never have KNOWN if it wasn't for..." Shifty pointed to the floor, "that cat."

When Shifty had tugged the plant off the
fridge – which he'd *thought* was the robber's
bushy beard – the plant had knocked off the
bug-eyed *cat*, which had fallen on Sam's *head*
and WOKEN him!

"This means—" said Shifty.

"I know!" grinned Sam.

"Brian IS lucky!

Told you!"

Sam promised not to snaffle ANY more
cheese.

"I am really hungry though," he said.

Come to think of it, Shifty was too. He
reached down the cookie jar.

"Oooo!" beamed Sam.
"Two *chocolate* ones
left – now that's
VERY lucky!"